300L

R0201727690

12/2020

W9-AYO-574

MAX & MO

Make a Snowman

For another set of best friends,
Max and Mia—P. L.

For Patricia Lakin,
with thanks—B. F.

SIMON SPOTLIGHT
An imprint of Simon & Schuster Children's Publishing Division
1230 Avenue of the Americas, New York, NY 10020
This Simon Spotlight edition December 2020
First Simon Spotlight edition December 2007
Text copyright © 2007 by Patricia Lakin
Illustrations copyright © 2007 by Brian Floca
All rights reserved, including the right of reproduction in
whole or in part in any form.
SIMON SPOTLIGHT, READY-TO-READ, and colophon are registered
trademarks of Simon & Schuster, Inc.
For information about special discounts for bulk purchases,
please contact Simon & Schuster Special Sales at
1-866-506-1949 or business@simonandschuster.com.
Manufactured in the United States of America 1020 LAK
2 4 6 8 10 9 7 5 3 1
Library of Congress Cataloging-in-Publication Number 2007002726
ISBN 978-1-5344-8071-1 (hc)
ISBN 978-1-4169-2537-8 (pbk)
ISBN 978-1-5344-0035-1 (eBook)

MAX & MO
Make a Snowman

By Patricia Lakin
Illustrated by Brian Floca

Simon Spotlight

New York   London   Toronto   Sydney   New Delhi

Max and Mo were
best friends.
They loved to curl up
in their cozy cage . . .

. . . in the art room
to watch the big ones.

"What are they making?"
asked Max.

Mo read the sign.
"Snowflakes," he said.

"Like those?" Max pointed.

"SNOW!" the big ones cheered.
"Let's go outside!" said the
biggest one.
Hats and mittens flew.

Mo climbed up.

He pulled
Max up.

"Look!" said Max.
"They are making a snowman."

"We will make one too,"
said Mo.

"Go outside," said Mo.

"Too cold!" they said.

They ran back inside.

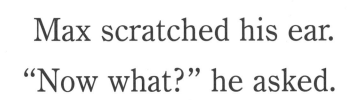

Max scratched his ear.
"Now what?" he asked.

Mo scratched his chin.
He saw a bin.

"Dive in!"

Paper and glue flew.

Cups, seeds, and yarn too.

"But we have no snow,"
said Max.

"We do not need snow,"
said Mo.
"We need white circles."

"Trace this!" said Max.

They made three circles.

They cut.

They taped.

"Look!" said Max.
"Their snowman can stand up."
Mo scratched his chin.

They taped their circles to a tube.

"Now ours can too!"

"Look!" said Max.
"Their snowman can see
and smile."
Mo scratched his chin.

They glued
on seeds.

"Now ours can see
and smile!"

"And our snowman will get
a hat," said Mo.

"And a scarf!" said Max.

"And arms!" they said.

"We made a great snowman!"

Max and Mo curled up
with their snowman
in their warm, cozy cage.

Want to make a snowman?

Here is what you will need:

1. A grown-up's help
2. Paper
3. Scissors
4. Pencil
5. Tape
6. Paste
7. Seeds, raisins, or peppercorns
8. Yarn or ribbon
9. Two toothpicks
10. Cup
11. Black paint or marker
12. Egg carton
13. Paper towel tube
14. Ruler

Here is how:

1. Trace

2. Cut

3. Tape

4. Measure

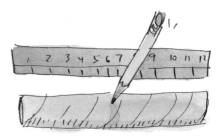

5. Cut

6. Tape

7. Paste

8. Cut

9. Paint

10. Paste

11. Tie

12. Tape